Ruby's Cupcakes

Grosset & Dunlap
An Imprint of Penguin Group (USA) Inc.

Based upon the animated series Max & Ruby
A Nelvana Limited production © 2002–2003.

Max & Ruby™ and © Rosemary Wells. Licensed by Nelvana Limited NELVANA™ Nelvana Limited. CORUS™ Corus Entertainment Inc. All Rights Reserved. Used under license by Penguin Young Readers Group. Published in 2011 by Grosset & Dunlap, a division of Penguin Young Readers Group, 345 Hudson Street, New York, New York 10014. GROSSET & DUNLAP is a trademark of Penguin Group (USA) Inc. Printed in the U.S.A.

ISBN 978-0-448-45594-5   10 9 8 7 6 5 4 3 2 1

"Grandma, thank you for helping me bake cupcakes," said Ruby. "They will be the hit of the Bunny Scout Bake Sale!"

"You're welcome," Grandma told her. "See you later at the bake sale."

"Max," said Ruby, "please don't play in here. I need to make posters to let people know about today's bake sale."

"Plane?" Max said.

"I can't play now, Max. Take your plane outside," said Ruby. "I have work to do."

Ruby started to paint her posters.
Suddenly, Max's Skydiver Plane flew in!
Luckily it didn't smudge her paint . . .

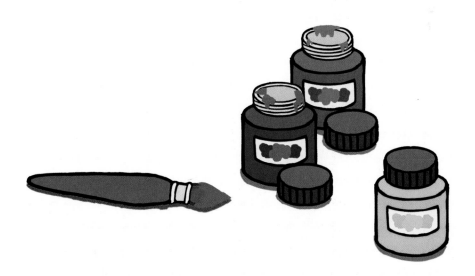

But it did land in the bowl of icing!
"Max, please take that plane outside!"
said Ruby.

Max left the kitchen. He wanted to get more planes.

Then Ruby went back to painting her poster.

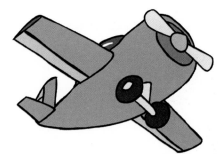

Whoosh!

Suddenly, something flew right by Ruby. It was Max's Skymaster Stealth Jet.

It blew Ruby's wet poster onto a clean piece of paper.

"Oh no! My poster is ruined!" cried Ruby.

When Ruby peeled the papers apart, she saw that she had two perfect posters! "Wow," Ruby said. "I can make lots of posters if I stamp them together like this!"

It didn't take Ruby long to make all her posters.

Once the paint was dry, it was time to hang the posters around town.

Ruby was going to use Max's wagon to carry all the posters.

But Max had another idea. He attached one of Ruby's posters to his Rescue Helicopter.

"Max, this is no time to play with your planes!" cried Ruby.

20

But then Max flew the poster right over to Grandma's house.

"If we fly the posters around town, everyone will know about the bake sale in no time!" Ruby said.

So Max attached one poster to each of his planes. Then he flew them all over town.

Soon, everyone was headed to the Bunny Scout Bake Sale.

"Yum!" said Valerie.

"Delicious," added Rosalinda. "I'm so glad I got your poster."

"Well," said Ruby, "I couldn't have done it without Max's sweet idea!"